JOIN THE ✓ SO-AZT-096
IN CABIN SIX . . .

KATIE is the perfect team player. She loves competitive games, planned activities, and coming up with her own great ideas.

MEGAN would rather lose herself in fantasyland than get into organized fun.

SARAH would be much happier if she could spend her time reading instead of exerting herself.

ERIN is much more interested in boys, clothes, and makeup than in playing kids' games at camp.

TRINA hates conflicts. She just wants everyone to be happy . . .

AND THEY ARE! Despite all their differences, the Cabin Six bunch are having the time of their lives at CAMP SUNNYSIDE!

The Problem With Parents

Marilyn Kaye

AN AVON CAMELOT BOOK

CAMP SUNNYSIDE FRIENDS #11: THE PROBLEM WITH PARENTS is an original publication of Avon Books. This work has never before appeared in book form.

AVON BOOKS
A division of
The Hearst Corporation
1350 Avenue of the Americas
New York, New York 10019

First Avon Camelot Printing: April 1991

CAMELOT TRADEMARK REG. U.S. PAT. OFF. AND IN OTHER COUNTRIES, MARCA REGISTRADA, HECHO EN U.S.A.

Printed in the U.S.A.

OPM 10 9 8 7 6 5 4 3 2

For Kibbie Ruth

Chapter 1

In the dining hall at Camp Sunnyside, the girls at the cabin six table attacked their breakfasts with gusto. At least, most of them did.

"Trina, aren't you going to eat anything?" Sarah asked after a while.

Trina looked down and realized she'd barely touched the golden-brown waffles on her plate. "I guess I'm not all that hungry," she replied.

Carolyn, their counselor, looked up. "Are you feeling all right, Trina?"

"I'm absolutely fine," Trina assured her. Physically, that was true. It was her mind that kept her from eating. Excitement had completely killed her appetite.

Her best friend, Katie, caught her eye and

1

winked knowingly. *She* knew why Trina couldn't eat. And the others would find out eventually.

Sarah couldn't take her eyes off Trina's waffles. "If you're not going to eat those . . ."

Trina lifted her plate and extended it across the table. "They're all yours."

Erin raised her eyebrows as Sarah accepted the plate. "Do you know how many calories are in one waffle?"

"Oh, leave her alone," Megan said mildly. "Sarah can have seconds if she wants. She's lost tons of weight since camp started. She's not even chubby anymore."

"But she will be if she eats double portions of waffles every morning," Erin pointed out.

"We don't get waffles every morning," Sarah replied. "Please pass the syrup."

Erin sighed deeply and shook her head. "You'll be sorry," she said darkly. The others ignored her. They were all accustomed to Erin's criticisms of their figures, hair, clothes, everything that had anything to do with a person's appearance. Trina recalled being told many times how she should change her hairstyle and let her fingernails grow.

But that was Erin's way. She was so intensely

concerned with her own looks, she couldn't understand why the others weren't. But they all had more important things on their minds. At least, Trina did.

"Good morning, campers."

Trina, along with all the other kids in the dining hall, turned toward the front of the room where the camp director stood, looking a little more flustered than usual.

"I know you're all looking forward to Parents' Day tomorrow," Ms. Winkle began. "And you're very excited about seeing your moms and dads. As you know, we're not having any special events this year. We think it would be nice for your parents to observe your regular routine and see what a typical day at Camp Sunnyside is like."

Megan spoke softly so only the cabin six table could hear her. "Wow, I'll bet they're going to get a big kick out of seeing us make our beds."

Katie grinned. "Yeah, not to mention watching us lying on our beds during quiet time."

"Hush, girls," Carolyn scolded them. "Listen to Ms. Winkle."

"But even though we're not planning anything out of the ordinary, that doesn't mean we shouldn't show our best faces tomorrow."

3

"Gee, I'm sorry," Megan whispered, "but this is the only face I've got."

Once again, Carolyn gave her a reproving look, but it was no use. Sarah's shoulders were shaking from suppressed laughter. Even Trina had to clap her hand over her mouth to keep the giggles from coming out.

Ms. Winkle went on to give her standard pep talk, with the usual comments on good attitudes and Sunnyside spirit. Since Trina had heard this speech many times before, she let her attention drift away and started thinking about what tomorrow might bring. If everything went according to her plan, tomorrow could turn out to be the best day of her life. But if everything didn't work out—she pushed that possibility aside and refused to even consider it.

"So let's show your parents that a typical Sunnyside day is a wonderful day," Ms. Winkle finished.

"Or else they might not send us back here next summer," Katie added. The girls all burst out laughing.

"Now come on," Carolyn remonstrated. "I'll bet you all really are excited about seeing your parents tomorrow."

"I'm not," Erin said with a grimace.

"Oh, Erin, I'm sorry," Carolyn said quickly. "I forgot that your parents are in Europe."

Erin shook her head. "They're back from Europe. And they're coming."

"Then what are you so down about?" Sarah asked.

"Because I know how they act when they haven't seen me for a while. They'll treat me like an infant. Especially my mother. She gets so mushy."

"I wouldn't complain if I were you," Sarah said. "At least you've *got* a mother."

An awkward silence fell over the table. Trina remembered that Sarah's mother was dead. Impulsively, she leaned across the table and laid her own hand gently on Sarah's.

Sarah flushed. "Hey, it's okay. I mean, she died when I was a baby. I don't even remember her. I'm just saying Erin should appreciate having a mother."

Trina nodded in agreement. *She* certainly appreciated hers, and she missed her vivacious, slightly scatterbrained mother. She appreciated her father, too—even though he didn't live with them.

"I appreciate her," Erin said indignantly. "It's just that sometimes she forgets that I'm

5

twelve years old. But she did lend me her pearls to bring to camp. That was pretty cool."

"Pearls at summer camp," Katie muttered, rolling her eyes. "Hey, Sarah, how come your father never got married again?"

"Katie!" Carolyn exclaimed. "That's very personal and none of your business."

"He'd never get married," Sarah stated. "Why should he? He's got me and my sister, so he's not lonely. Besides us, the only other thing he cares about is his work."

"He's a doctor, isn't he?" Carolyn asked.

Sarah nodded proudly. "And he's real important. Practically famous. He's doing some serious research, trying to find a cure for a terrible disease. Other doctors call him all the time for advice."

"Wouldn't you like him to get married again?" Megan asked. "Then you'd have a mother."

Sarah shrugged. "Not particularly. We're happy just the way we are. I don't need a new mother." She turned to Trina. "Would you want a new father?"

"Good grief, no!" Trina said. "Why would I want a new father? I've already got one."

"But they're divorced, right?"

"Well, yeah, but . . ." Trina decided it was time to change the subject. "Katie, your parents are coming, aren't they?"

"Sure, they'll be here. They never miss a Parents' Day."

In a too-casual tone, Erin asked, "Are the boys coming with them?"

"No, thank goodness," Katie declared. "Sorry about that, Erin." But her expression made it very clear that she didn't feel the least bit sorry.

Everyone exchanged knowing looks as Erin's face fell. Trina remembered how Erin had flirted with Katie's twin brothers at Katie's Christmas reunion house party. Thinking about that week, Trina smiled. The reunion had been so much fun. Katie was very lucky to have a real family, with two parents. It was with a pang that Trina recalled having that once herself.

"C'mon, Trina," Katie called.

Trina hadn't even noticed that the other girls had already returned their trays and were heading for the door. She jumped up and hurried after them.

Carolyn walked behind the others with Trina. "Who do you have coming tomorrow?" she asked. "Your mother or your father?"

Trina hesitated. Then she figured she might

as well tell. Carolyn would find out tomorrow anyway. "Both of them."

She couldn't blame Carolyn for looking surprised. In the past, either her mother or her father came on camp visiting days—never both. "Really?"

Trina nodded. "I wrote them both and invited them."

"Do they both know the other one's coming?"

Trina shook her head. "I don't think so. At least, I didn't tell them I was asking both of them in my letters." Actually, that was part of her plan. She'd been afraid that if they did know she'd invited both of them, one of them wouldn't come.

Carolyn gazed at her in concern. "Trina, do you think that's a good idea? You told me your parents haven't been on the best of terms since their divorce."

Trina kicked a stone along as she walked. "That's because they don't try to get along. They never even see each other anymore." She sighed. "His lawyer calls her lawyer and her lawyer calls his lawyer." She gave her stone an especially fierce kick and sent it flying.

Carolyn didn't say anything, and Trina gave her a sidelong look. The counselor seemed concerned, as if she was trying to decide what to say. Luckily, just then another counselor came toward them. "Carolyn, do you have a minute?"

"Be right with you," Carolyn said. "Trina . . . do you want to talk about this?"

"Thanks, but there's nothing really to talk about," Trina said. "I just want them to get along better. I'm not expecting anything else."

As she ran on to join the others, she hoped her face wasn't flushed. She'd never been very good at lying. But she had a pretty good idea what Carolyn would say if Trina told what her real motives were.

In the cabin, the girls were busily making their beds and generally straightening up. They were putting a little more energy into their efforts than usual.

Megan was on the floor, peering beneath her bunk. "If my mother sees this mess under my bed, she'll have a fit." Looking like a red-haired snake, she slithered under the bed.

"You really think she'll look under your bed?" Sarah asked. She was standing on the ladder, plumping the pillow on her upper bunk.

Megan emerged with three socks and a tennis ball. "Well, it's the first place she looks in my room at home."

9

Trina took a quick look under her bed. As she expected, there was nothing there. Above her, Katie was smoothing her sheets. "I think my mom goes over my room with a magnifying glass. She finds things I didn't even know were there."

Erin casually tossed her bedspread over her sheets. "*I* don't have to worry about stuff like that. We have a maid at home to clean up."

"Gee, it must be really tough for you here," Katie said, her voice dripping with fake sympathy.

Climbing down from the ladder, Sarah eyed Trina's bed and nightstand with envy. "How do you keep everything so neat? I could stand absolutely still in a room and it would turn into a mess."

Trina laughed. "I guess it just comes naturally to me. I like having everything neat and clean and in its place."

Katie glanced down at her. "I'll bet your mother never complains about your room."

"Never," Trina said. "In fact, it's usually me picking up after her and scolding her for making a mess. You should see her desk. It's so cluttered, I don't know how she finds anything."

"I've never heard of a mother being a slob," Erin commented.

"She's not a slob," Trina corrected her. "A little messy, that's all. She'll have something on her mind, and she just doesn't see anything around her."

"She sounds like Megan," Katie said.

Megan didn't look the least bit offended. She knew she was famous for having her head in the clouds.

"There's a difference," Trina said. "My mother isn't a daydreamer. She just gets very caught up in her work."

"Like my father," Sarah remarked. "What kind of work does your mother do?"

"She's a writer," Trina told her. "She writes articles for magazines and newspapers."

Sarah was impressed. "Wow. I'd really like to talk to her about that."

"Well, maybe you'll get a chance tomorrow," Trina said. "But I'm hoping she'll spend most of the day talking to my father." That slipped out before she could stop herself.

"Hey, that was supposed to be our secret!" Katie exclaimed.

"Well, they're going to see him here," Trina replied.

Megan's eyes widened. "Your father's coming too?"

"But won't that be weird?" Erin asked. "They're *divorced.*"

Trina concentrated on tucking in her sheets under the mattress. "Well, they are *now.* But you never know."

"You mean, you think they might get back together?" Megan asked excitedly. "Right here at Sunnyside? Oh, Trina, that would be so romantic!"

"That's her plan," Katie piped up.

Trina nodded happily. "I figured if I could bring them together, in person, they'd *have* to talk to each other. And once they started talking, they'd realize they still love each other."

"Get real, Trina," Erin said in a know-it-all way. "If they loved each other, they wouldn't have gotten divorced in the first place."

A sudden lump formed in Trina's throat and she couldn't speak. Katie jumped to her defense. "That's not necessarily true. You can have a fight with your best friend and absolutely hate her one day. But then you make up and you're best friends again. It happens all the time."

Trina found her voice. "That's what I think too. Deep inside, I'll bet they still love each other. All they need is a little push, and every-thing could go back the way it used to be, before they started fighting and all that. I just want them both to be happy."

"And then you'd be happy too," Katie mur-mured.

Trina smiled. "More than happy."

Carolyn came into the cabin. "Okay, inspec-tion time."

The girls lined up by their bunks while Car-olyn walked the length of the cabin. "Honestly, Erin, a person would think you've never made a bed before."

Katie whispered in Trina's ear. "Maybe next summer she can get permission to bring her maid with her."

"Get into your bathing suits," Carolyn told them when she finished inspection. "You don't want to be late for your swimming class."

Just then, there was a knock on the door. Car-olyn opened it and stuck her head out. The girls couldn't hear what the person outside was say-ing, but when Carolyn closed the door she looked a little puzzled. "Trina, you're wanted in Ms. Winkle's office."

"Me? Ms. Winkle wants to see me?"

"That's what I've just been told."

"But why?" Trina asked.

"I haven't the slightest idea," Carolyn replied. "But you're supposed to go there right away."

Katie clutched Trina's arm. "What did you do?"

Trina was totally bewildered. "Nothing!"

"You don't get called to Ms. Winkle's office for doing nothing," Erin said. "You must have broken some rule."

"That's ridiculous," Katie said. "Trina doesn't break rules. Not like *some* people," she added, looking pointedly at Erin.

"Now, let's not jump to conclusions," Carolyn said. "We don't know why Ms. Winkle wants to see Trina. It doesn't necessarily mean she's in trouble."

"That's true," Megan said thoughtfully. "It could mean there's an emergency back home."

"Megan!" Carolyn exclaimed.

Now Trina was frightened. "Maybe something's happened to my mother!"

"Don't get upset," Carolyn said soothingly. "There's no point in trying to guess why Ms. Winkle wants to see you. Just run along and find out."

14

"Do you want me to go with you?" Katie asked.

Trina shook her head. If bad news was coming, she'd just as soon be alone when she heard it. "Thanks anyway." She got up, threw back her shoulders, and walked out of the cabin.

She walked briskly, looking straight ahead. But inside, her stomach was jumping and she was thankful she hadn't eaten those waffles. Her mind raced through every minute of every recent day. What could she have possibly done wrong?

Nothing. She was sure of it. In three years at Sunnyside, she'd never even had a demerit. So there had to be another reason why the camp director wanted to see her.

Horrible visions filled her head. Her mother, lying in a hospital bed. Her house burning down. A car accident . . .

Her step quickened, and before long she was running. By the time she reached Ms. Winkle's office, she was out of breath. She paused for a moment outside the building to take some deep breaths. Then she opened the door.

The director was in the outer office, talking to her secretary at the reception desk. When she saw Trina, she smiled. This calmed Trina a little. Surely Ms. Winkle wouldn't smile if anything really terrible had happened.

"Did—did you want to see me?" Trina asked.

"No," Ms. Winkle replied. "But someone else does. Go on into my office, dear."

Puzzled, Trina went past the desk and pushed the director's office door open. When she saw who was already in there, she gasped.

"Daddy!"

Chapter 2

The tall, slender man opened his arms and Trina ran into them. After a tight hug, he released her and held her at arm's length.

"Now, let me look at my lovely daughter. Trina, I think you've grown another inch!"

"I must take after you," Trina said, thinking of her petite mother.

"You certainly do," he agreed fondly. "Same hair, same eyes, but you're turning into a beautiful young lady."

"And you're the handsomest father in the world," Trina replied promptly. "That's not just my opinion either! All my cabin mates said that the last time you visited."

Her father's brown eyes twinkled. "I'm glad

17

to know you've got such intelligent cabin mates."

Trina laughed. "Oh, Daddy, I'm so happy to see you. But what are you doing here *today?* Parents' Day is tomorrow!"

"I called your Ms. Winkle and got special permission to come today."

"Great!" Trina exclaimed. "Then I'll have you for two days instead of just one!"

His smile faded slightly. Then he shook his head. "No, honey, I'm just here for today. I'll be driving back downstate tonight."

Trina's face fell. "But why do you need to go back? Tomorrow's Sunday. You don't have to go to work."

Mr. Sandburg looked oddly uncomfortable. Folding his arms across his chest, he leaned back against Ms. Winkle's desk and gazed down at the floor for a second. When he raised his eyes, they were serious. "I found out that your mother is planning to come to camp tomorrow. And I thought it would be more . . . more appropriate if I came today instead."

Now it was Trina's turn to stare at the floor. She blinked rapidly to keep tears from forming. When she felt like she had her feelings under control, she looked back at him and managed a small smile.

"Did you talk to her?" she asked hopefully.

"No. A mutual friend of ours happened to mention it."

"Oh." It was getting impossible to stop the tears. Even biting her lip didn't help. She lowered her eyes again, but her father must have seen something there. He came forward and put his arm around her.

"Trina, don't be upset. You must know that whenever your mother and I talk, we just start arguing. And then we both get upset. It's not very pleasant."

Trina knew that was true. But it didn't make her feel any better.

When her father spoke again, his voice was gentle. "Honey, why did you invite both of us on the same day anyway? You usually let us take turns visiting."

Trina didn't trust herself to speak. She was afraid her voice would break. She just shrugged.

He went on. "I hope you didn't have some scheme in mind to get us back together. We won't, and you know that. I realize that it's hard for you to accept, Trina, but that's the way it is. You have to understand that."

Trina took a deep breath. "I don't even understand why you got divorced in the first place."

"I find that hard to believe," Mr. Sandburg said. "You have to remember all the arguing at home. Look, Trina, divorce is a terrible thing. No one wants it to happen. But sometimes it's for the best."

Trina looked at him in disbelief. "Divorce—the best?"

He nodded. "Your mother and I married very young. Over the years, we both changed. And we grew apart. Believe me, Trina, it's better this way. We're both feeling much better now than we did when we were married."

Trina heard the words, but she refused to believe them. Okay, maybe her parents did fight a lot. So what? She'd had fights with Katie, and sometimes she felt like she never wanted to speak to her again. But they always made up in the end. Her parents just weren't even trying.

He stroked her hair. "Of course, it's nicer to have two parents in the same house. But which would you rather have—two parents living together who are miserable, or two parents living apart who are happy?"

20

Trina knew the answer to that. "Two parents living together who are happy."

"Oh, honey, I'm afraid you can't have that. But at least you can know that your mother and I have one thing in common."

"What's that?"

"We both love you very much."

It wasn't much comfort. But Trina nodded anyway and said, "I know that."

"No more tears," Mr. Sandburg said briskly. "Let's put all these sad feelings aside and have a nice day."

"What are we going to do?" Trina asked.

"First of all, we're driving into Pine Ridge and having a little shopping spree. I've got a credit card in my pocket that seems to be calling your name."

Despite herself, Trina's lips twitched. Her father could be so funny.

Encouraged, her father continued. "We're going to hit the record store, the bookstore, and some of those little shops I noticed in town that are displaying the latest fashions. The sky's the limit! How does that sound to you?"

Like a bribe, Trina thought. To make up for refusing to even see my mother. "Fine," she said.

He didn't seem to notice her indifference. Or maybe he was just pretending not to notice. "Then we'll have a nice lunch at the best restaurant in town. After that . . ." he paused to think. "I saw a bowling alley and a skating rink. Do those appeal to you? Or maybe you just want to do more shopping?"

"We can do anything you want," Trina said.

"Anything *you* want," Mr. Sandburg corrected her.

Trina just shrugged again. "Sure."

Her father sighed. "Honey, don't be like that. I really want this to be a nice day."

He sounded so sincere, so truly caring, that it was irresistible. Trina forced herself to give him a smile. "Okay, Dad. It'll be a nice day."

They left the office. Ms. Winkle smiled at them brightly. "Have a nice day!"

Trina and her father exchanged looks and started laughing. As Ms. Winkle stared after them in puzzlement, Trina called, "Thank you," and they left the building.

Trina glanced down at her shorts and tee shirt. "If we're having lunch in the best restaurant, I'd better change my clothes." She led her father to cabin six.

Since it was still swimming period, the cabin

was empty. Mr. Sandburg waited outside while Trina went inside and pulled a skirt and blouse from the closet.

As she dressed, she tried not to feel too depressed by the fact that her little scheme had been totally messed up. It wasn't the end of the world. It might not even be the end of her scheme! She and her father would have a fine day together. And maybe he'd have such a good time with her, that he'd decide to stay for Parents' Day after all.

She ran a brush through her hair and went back outside. "All set for a day on the town?" her father asked.

"All ready," Trina replied. "And I'm looking forward to this."

"That's the spirit!" Mr. Sandburg said as they headed down to the main road.

"Where's your car?" Trina asked.

Her father pointed. "Right there."

Trina gasped. It wasn't the familiar station wagon. "Dad, you bought a new car!"

"What do you think of it?" he asked proudly.

Trina wasn't sure. The jazzy little red sports car was undeniably gorgeous. But a two-seater certainly wasn't a family car. They got in, and Mr. Sandburg started the engine.

"It's very nice," Trina said politely. Then, to make up for her lack of enthusiasm, she quickly added, "I'm glad we're having this day together, Dad. Just the two of us."

Now he looked *really* uncomfortable. As he pulled the car onto the road, he said, "Well, Trina, it's not going to be just the two of us. Not for the whole day. You see . . ." He seemed to be struggling for words. And his face was beginning to turn pink."There's somebody joining us for lunch."

"Okay," Trina said. It was probably one of his business associates, she thought. That happened sometimes during weekends back home. She suspected that her father was turning into what they called a workaholic. It would be boring, listening to them talk about stocks and bonds or whatever. But she could spend the time planning subtle ways to bring up the subject of her mother.

"I don't mind," she said. "Is it one of those bank people?"

"Not exactly."

Trina looked at him curiously. Now his face was beet red. "I mean, she *does* work in a bank, but . . ."

"But what?"

He kept his eyes on the road as he spoke. "It's not a business relationship. This is a woman I've . . . I've been seeing."

"Seeing," Trina repeated. Despite the warm sun streaming in through the open window, a cold chill went through her. She shivered. "What do you mean, seeing?" she asked, knowing perfectly well what that word implied.

"Dating," he said, confirming her fears.

Trina swallowed. She knew that her father dated women. Sometimes, when she stayed at his apartment, one of them would call. But he never talked about any of them. He never tried to introduce them to Trina.

Her mother had had a few dates too, over the past year. But they hadn't meant anything special to her.

Trina tried to keep her voice steady as she asked the question she dreaded hearing the answer to. "Why do you want me to meet her?"

"Well, we're . . . we're very fond of each other. I've told her a lot about you. She's anxious to meet you."

Trina certainly couldn't say the same about her, whoever she was. "That's nice," she said dully.

"I guess I should tell you about her," her father said.

"If you want."

"Her name is Shelly Fowler. She's an assistant manager at one of the banks I work with. She's very nice, Trina. She has a lively personality, she's intelligent, and she's got a great sense of humor."

So does Mom, Trina thought. Aloud, she said, "And I'll bet she's beautiful."

"She's very pretty," he said. "Actually, I think she looks a little like you! Maybe that's what attracted me to her." He reached over and ruffled Trina's hair.

Trina pushed his hand away.

"Oh, Trina, don't be like that," he pleaded. "You want your mother and me to be happy, don't you?"

"Of course I do," Trina replied automatically. Silently, she added, happy with each other.

"If you just give her a chance," Mr. Sandburg continued, "I think you'll like her."

Trina wiped a bead of perspiration from her forehead. Her stomach was churning, and she had to force the next words out. "Are you going to marry her?"

He took his time before answering. "There's nothing definite yet."

Yet. That one word alone sent her head to the window. She couldn't bear to look at him.

"Trina, I hope you're not upset."

"I'm not upset." Trina marveled at her ability to keep her voice steady. "Just surprised, that's all. I didn't know you were seeing anyone like that."

She could hear the misery in her father's voice. "I probably shouldn't have sprung it on you like that. But I didn't know what else to do."

"It's okay," Trina said. But she kept her eyes on the view out the window. She had to think. This information considerably altered her plans.

She didn't get much time to think. Her father pulled into Main Street, Pine Ridge, and parked the car.

They did everything he'd promised. The record store first, where he bought Trina every album she looked at. The same happened at the bookstore.

"We'll have to hit the boutiques after lunch," he said as they emerged from the bookstore with their bags. "I told Shelly we'd meet her at twelve-thirty."

27

He led Trina to the Golden Palm, a restaurant she and her cabin mates had passed many times during their trips to Pine Ridge. Its windows were heavily curtained, and the door was very fancy. They'd always wondered what it was like inside. At least now she'd have a chance to find out.

"Sandburg," her father told the man at the little desk inside. "Reservations for three."

The man led them toward the back of the restaurant. A woman was already sitting at the table, and Trina had a moment to size her up before they reached her.

Her hair was short, straight, and dark brown. Trina couldn't make out the color of her eyes, but they were large. Trina didn't think she looked the least bit like *her,* despite what her father had said. As they approached, she rose, and Trina could see that she was small, like her mother. At least he still likes the same size woman, she thought.

"Trina, this is Shelly Fowler. Shelly, this is my daughter, Trina."

Trina extended her right hand. "How do you do."

The woman grasped her hand in both of hers.

"Oh, Trina, I'm very glad to meet you. I've heard so much about you!"

Trina smiled thinly and sat down.

It was a strange meal. Not the food—that was okay. Better than okay, really. Trina only wished she had more of an appetite, so she could do her lamb chops justice. But it was hard to chew, even harder to swallow. She just felt too awful.

What made everything really horrible was that this Shelly person was *nice*. Trina wanted to dislike her, maybe even hate her. But how could she hate someone who showed so much interest in everything about her?

"Your father told me you've been coming to this camp for three years," she said. "You must like it."

"Yes," Trina said.

"Tell me about it," Shelly urged. "What do you do each day?"

Reluctantly, Trina related the average day's activities. "There's swimming, arts and crafts, archery, horseback riding, and lakefront stuff, like canoes and sailboats."

"And color wars," her father prompted her.

"Oh, yeah," Trina said. "That's the annual summer competition, where the campers are divided into two colors and we have different events. And the Sunnyside Spectacular, where we put on skits."

She didn't really feel like saying much more, but that anxious expression on her father's face made her relent. "Once, we put on an original play, that one of the girls in my cabin wrote."

"Did you play a part in it?" Shelly asked.

Trina poked her rice with her fork. "No. I worked on the sets."

Shelly smiled broadly. "That's exactly what I would have done!" She leaned across the table toward Trina with an air of confidence. "I've always had stage fright. I'd never want to perform in front of people."

Trina started to grin, but she caught herself just in time. "I don't mind performing in front of people," she lied. "I just like painting better."

"Tell Trina about your job at the bank," Mr. Sandburg urged Shelly.

As Shelly complied, Trina tuned her out. She spent the next few minutes counting the grains of rice on her plate.

By the time they were finished eating, Trina felt like there was nothing she'd rather do more than leave immediately and spend the rest of the day alone in cabin six. But she still had the rest of the day to spend with her father.

"What would you like to do?" he asked her. "Bowling, skating, or more shopping?"

Trina really didn't care. "Bowling's fine."

"I love bowling!" Shelly exclaimed.

Trina's father looked at Trina with raised eyebrows. And natural politeness forced Trina to invite Shelly to go bowling with them.

They all went across the street to the bowling alley. Trina had been there many times before with the cabin six girls. But she'd never bowled a worse game in her life. And she'd never felt so crummy playing.

"That was fun!" Shelly said as they left.

"Yeah," Trina murmured.

"When you get back from camp," Shelly continued, "I hope we'll see lots of each other."

Trina looked at her father, an unspoken question in her eyes. But her father didn't seem to notice.

Shelly left them at the car. Trina watched as her father had a whispered conversation with her. She was actually grateful that the car was only a two-seater. At least, Shelly wouldn't be able to ride back to Sunnyside with them.

"What do you think of Shelly?" Mr. Sandburg asked eagerly as they drove away.

"She's very nice," Trina said.

"I'm glad you think so," her father said. "I want you two to be friends."

Trina didn't bother to ask why. She knew the answer. "I'm kind of tired," she murmured. She leaned back in her seat, closed her eyes, and pretended to be asleep.

She wasn't really sleepy. But she didn't want to answer any more questions about Shelly. She wanted to think about her mother coming to-morrow. At least, she still had *her*.

She had a feeling she'd lost her father.

Chapter 3

Everyone in cabin six got up just a little earlier than usual on Parents' Day. Even though they'd been taking special pains with the look of their cabin all week, this was their last chance to make sure they made the best impression on their guests.

Erin spent most of the time carefully applying makeup. Sarah was lining up books in a neat, precise row on the bookshelf, while Megan folded the clothes that were stuffed in her drawer.

Katie let out a groan as she worked on her bed. "This is silly. We're supposed to straighten up *after* breakfast. How can I work like this on an empty stomach?"

"But the parents will already be here by the regular cleanup time," Sarah noted. "Do you want them to see your bed like that?"

Katie grinned. "They've seen worse at home."

Trina finished making her bed. Then she climbed up the ladder to help Katie get her sheets tucked in tightly. "What time are your parents coming?" Trina asked.

"During breakfast," Katie said. "When's your mother going to be here?"

"Same time," Trina replied. "At least, that's when I told her to be here."

"It's too bad you couldn't get your father to stay," Katie remarked.

Trina made a face. "Why would he want to stay here with me when he can be with his girl-friend?" She practically spat out those last words, and Katie stared at her in astonishment.

"Trina! That doesn't sound like you!"

Trina bit her lip. Katie was right, and she felt ashamed. She'd never talked in such a nasty way about a person, especially one she barely knew. "Yeah, I'm sorry I said that. It's not really Shelly's fault. I can't blame her just because my father doesn't care about me or my mother anymore." She spoke in a low tone so the others wouldn't hear. And Katie responded in a whisper.

"I'm sure he still cares about you, Trina."

Trina shrugged. "I wonder if my mother knows about Shelly. She must be so hurt. I'm sure she's been thinking that she and Dad would get back together."

"Does she talk about that much?" Katie asked.

"No . . . but I'm positive she feels that way. My mother's not the kind of person who stops loving somebody." She shuddered. "Maybe she doesn't know he has a girlfriend, and *I'll* have to tell her."

Katie gazed at her in sympathy. "Yeah, that would be pretty awful."

"Not as awful as what *could* happen," Trina went on.

"What do you mean?"

Trina hesitated. She'd stayed awake late the night before conjuring up this horrible fantasy. Maybe if she actually expressed it, she'd feel better. "If he marries her, they'll probably have children. I mean, she's pretty young. Then he'd be all involved with his new family. And I'd never see him again."

It didn't make her feel better. And the look of

horror on Katie's face made her realize how truly possible that was. A wave of sadness filled her. "Oh, Katie, how could he desert me like that?"

"Well, it hasn't happened yet," Katie said. She reached over and gave Trina's hand a squeeze. "At least you still have your mother."

Trina nodded. It was a cheering thought. She wasn't completely alone. Maybe she couldn't count on her father anymore, but her mother would never desert her.

Carolyn came out of her room. "Wow, this place is spotless," she exclaimed. "I wish your parents would come more often."

"*I* don't," Megan said. "I'd collapse from all this work."

Carolyn rolled her eyes. "You look like you're in pretty good shape to me. Now, hurry up and get dressed. Your parents should be arriving soon and we want to be in the dining hall to greet them." She watched curiously as Erin applied yet another layer of shadow to eyelids that were already bright blue. "Erin, why are you wearing so much makeup?"

"I'm trying to look as old as possible," Erin told her. "Then maybe my mother won't treat me like a baby."

"Good luck," Carolyn said. "I'm a lot older than you, and my mother still treats me like a baby. All the makeup in the world won't make any difference."

"It's worth a try," Erin muttered.

Carolyn went around checking each of them. Finally, they were all ready, and set out for the dining hall.

Sarah was skipping, and practically giddy with excitement. "I can't wait to see my father," she told Trina. "And I'm kind of glad my older sister's not coming so I can have him all to myself." She stopped suddenly. "Oh! I'm sorry, Trina. I shouldn't be talking like that when your father . . ." Her voice trailed away in embarrassment.

"That's okay," Trina said. "I'm excited about seeing my mother."

"You know," Sarah said thoughtfully, "I think that when you live with just one parent, you get closer to that parent than kids do who have two parents."

Trina had to agree. She felt like she missed her mother more than most kids missed their parents.

The dining hall was even noisier than usual. Some parents had already arrived, and the room was alive with shrieks and hugs. Katie's parents and Megan's parents came at almost the same time. Trina watched enviously as Katie and Megan led them to get their breakfasts.

Sarah's father arrived soon after. Sarah was clinging tō his hand, taking him around to greet the others. "Hello, Dr. Fine," Trina said. "It's nice to see you again." He shook her hand and told her it was a pleasure to see her too. But as they spoke, Trina kept her eyes glued to the entrance.

Erin's parents came next. Her mother, wearing an elegant white suit and trailing clouds of perfume, swept through the crowd and practically lunged at poor Erin. "My baby! My precious sweetie!" She smothered Erin in kisses.

Erin looked like she wanted to drop through a hole in the ground. Trina couldn't help smiling. So Carolyn was right. Makeup didn't change anything when it came to mothers and daughters.

But where was *her* mother? By now, everyone was sitting around the table, eating and talking. Trina had just started chewing on her fingernails when she saw her.

She leaped up and ran to greet her. "Mom!"

She threw her arms around her. "I was just getting worried about you!"

Her mother's merry laugh seemed to rise above the general noise around them. "Oh, darling, I'm sorry, but you know me. I missed the right exit off the expressway, and of course I'd gone miles beyond before I realized what I'd done and turned back."

That was so typical of her, Trina thought in affection. "Mom, you're such a space cadet. I don't know how you manage at home without me."

Mrs. Sandburg bent down and kissed Trina's forehead. "It isn't easy. I miss you so much."

"I miss you too, Mom," Trina said with so much fervor that her mother seemed almost taken aback. They joined the other cabin six families at the table. "Mom, you know everyone. Why don't you sit down and I'll get our breakfasts."

When she returned with the two trays, her mother was talking to Dr. Fine, who was sitting on one side of her. "That's so fascinating," she was saying as Trina sat down on her other side. "Trina, did you know that Dr. Fine is doing extraordinary medical research?"

"Yes, Sarah told me." Trina really didn't

want to spend her one day with her mother hearing about Dr. Fine's research. "Mom, tell me what you've been up to. Are you writing something now?"

"Yes, a very boring and tedious political series for the newspaper. It's almost finished, thank goodness. I hope I can find something more interesting to do next, but I can't seem to come up with a good idea. I'd rather hear what you girls have been up to."

For the next half hour, she got her wish. The girls regaled her and the other parents with their exploits. After breakfast, they went back to the cabin.

"This looks wonderful!" Katie's mother exclaimed. "Do the girls really keep this place up by themselves?" she asked Carolyn.

Carolyn nodded and smiled. "With just a tiny bit of encouragement."

Megan's father laughed. "Are you sure you don't have to stand over them with a whip?"

"Oh, Dad," Megan groaned.

"I think it's excellent that the girls have to clean up after themselves," Mrs. Chapman, Erin's mother, announced. "It's important for them to understand how much work maids have to do."

Katie whispered in Trina's ear. "If there's a maid in our house, her name is Katie Dillon."

"Well, I'm impressed," Katie's mother said. "Carolyn, I wish we could hire you to come home with us to work your magic on Katie and the twins."

They went through the ritual of inspection, and then the parents went outside while the girls changed into their bathing suits.

"I hope we're diving today," Sarah said as they left the cabin. "I want to impress my father."

Trina lingered toward the back of the group so she could walk with her mother alone and have a few private moments. "Dad was here yesterday," she told her mother.

"I know. Did you two have a nice day together?"

"It was fine." Trina took a deep breath. She figured her mother might as well know. "He brought a girl to meet me. A woman, really."

To her surprise, her mother didn't seem disturbed. "Did you like her?"

"I guess she was okay. Mom . . ."

"What?"

"Do you think he's going to marry her?"

"I suppose it's possible. Does that idea bother you?"

Trina didn't answer. How could her mother talk so casually? Here Trina had just given her the worst possible news, and she was acting as if her only concern was for her daughter. Maybe she just couldn't bear to discuss it. Trina changed the subject. "Have you been going on dates?"

"Once in a while," she said. "But I haven't met anyone very interesting."

Trina's first reaction to that was relief. But then she felt concerned. "Have you been very lonely?"

"A little," Mrs. Sandburg admitted. "But mostly that's just because you're not around."

Trina put an arm around her. It was wonderful knowing she was still the most important person in her mother's life.

During swimming class, the parents stayed on the landing and watched while the girls showed off their skills. When the time came for diving, Trina, standing in line and waiting her turn, watched as Sarah took her place on the board. She was pleased to see her execute a perfect swan dive. When Sarah's head emerged from the water, she looked toward the landing with a gleeful expression. Then it was replaced by disappointment.

Trina turned and saw why. Sarah's father was deep in conversation with her own mother. Sarah climbed out of the pool. "Dad, you didn't see my dive!"

He was very apologetic. "I'm sorry, dear. Can you do it again?" Sarah got back in line. Fortunately, she was able to duplicate her performance, and she was rewarded with raves from her father.

After swimming, the girls went back to the cabin to change and then met their parents at the arts and crafts cabin. Much of the work the girls had done over the summer was displayed on the walls, and Trina took her mother around to point out her own art.

"You did this?" Mrs. Sandburg asked, admiring a collage. "This is lovely! It's so creative. I wish I had your talent."

"You're the creative one," Trina said. "You're a professional writer."

"I'm only creative with words," Mrs. Sandburg said. "I could never do anything like this. You must get this talent from your father. He used to dabble in painting."

"Let's not talk about *him*," Trina murmured.

Lines of concern crossed her mother's face. "Trina, don't be too hard on him," she said softly. "He's still your father and he's a good person. He deserves to be happy." She smiled brightly. "Cheer up, okay?"

Trina gazed at her in wonder. It was an awfully good act she was putting on. She was being so brave and noble, as if she didn't have a broken heart.

From arts and crafts, they went to archery. It had never been one of Trina's favorite sports, but she tried to concentrate so she could do well for her mother. It paid off. On her first attempt, she made a bull's-eye.

"Hey, Mom! Did you see that?" Trina turned around.

Apparently not. She was talking with Dr. Fine again.

When archery was over, they had lunch. Then the parents went to meet with Ms. Winkle while the girls had their rest period. As they were settling on their bunks, Sarah turned to Trina. "Your mother and my father are certainly talking a lot."

"Yeah, I saw that," Trina replied. "It's funny, I wouldn't have thought they'd have much in common to talk about."

"Maybe she's asking him about something medical," Sarah suggested.

"Is your mother sick?" Megan asked.

"Of course not," Trina said. But a sudden fear shot through her. Her mother *had* seemed awfully interested in talking to Dr. Fine. Could something be wrong that Trina didn't know about? Some awful disease?

She sat down on her bed, opened a magazine, and stared unseeing at the pages. She could feel herself breaking out in a cold sweat. No, it wasn't possible. She couldn't be sick.

But the second rest period was over, she ran out and raced ahead of the others to join her mother. "Where to now?" Mrs. Sandburg asked.

"The lakefront," Trina said. "We're taking canoes out." She studied her mother's face anxiously as they walked along. She *looked* healthy. "Mom, do you feel okay?"

"Of course I do. Why?"

"You're not sick or anything?"

Her mother looked at her strangely. "Darling, there's absolutely nothing wrong with me. I'd tell you if there was. What's this sudden interest in my health?"

"I just don't want anything bad to happen to you, Mom."

Mrs. Sandburg gave her a quick hug. "And I don't want anything bad to happen to you. Now, stop your worrying right this minute, okay? It's too beautiful a day to spend it fretting when nothing's wrong."

"Okay," Trina said. But she couldn't resist. "You promise me nothing's wrong with you?"

"I promise," her mother said.

A deep sigh of relief escaped Trina's lips. Her mother would never lie to her.

Down at the lakefront, they laid claim to a canoe. "I haven't been in one of these in years!" Mrs. Sandburg cried out with enthusiasm. She pulled off her shoes and left them on the bank. Then they dragged the canoe out into the water.

Trina couldn't help giggling as she watched Mrs. Chapman try to get into a canoe in her tight skirt. She was probably more accustomed to yachts. She noticed with pride the way her own mother gracefully climbed in, picked up a paddle, and started to row.

It was lovely out on the lake. For a few moments, Trina and her mother rowed in silence, just enjoying the quiet and the warm sun. "It's so nice up here in the country," her mother said. "I can see why you love camp."

"It *is* nice," Trina agreed. She felt as if she

was actually relaxing for the first time since her father's visit. She leaned back, and gave her paddle a lazy stroke. "Up here, it's like being in a different world. You're never bored, there's lots to do, and most of the kids are terrific."

"Mmm," her mother sighed. She rested her paddle and they drifted for a while. "I can just feel all the pressure and tension and stress draining out of my body. You can really escape all your problems in a place like this."

Trina became alert. She sat up so suddenly the canoe rocked. "What problems?"

"Just the usual ones," Mrs. Sandburg said. "Deadlines, dealing with editors. Trina, what *is* the matter? You're so jumpy!"

"It's nothing," Trina said quickly. "I just worry about you, that's all. Mom, I want you to be happy."

"Trina, I *am* happy." She closed her eyes and leaned back. "Right now, I'm absolutely ecstatic."

They drifted along some more, and then Mrs. Sandburg opened her eyes. "I've been thinking . . ."

"What, Mom?"

"I need to get away for a few days. And I saw

47

the cutest little inn in Pine Ridge. What would you think if I stayed on up here for a few days?"

Trina gasped in delight. "Mom, that's fabulous! But what about your work?"

Mrs. Sandburg waved a hand nonchalantly. "I'm a writer. I can write anywhere. And I love the idea of having a few more days with you. Of course, I won't interfere with your camp activities," she added quickly. "But maybe I can wangle a few special permissions from Ms. Winkle so we can get together."

Trina nodded happily. Just then, Sarah and her father in their canoe came alongside them. "Hey, want to race?" Sarah called out.

"You're on!" Mrs. Sandburg called back. She grabbed her paddle. "C'mon, Trina, let's show them what Sandburg girls are made of."

Trina took up her paddle, and they started slapping the water furiously. But even as she concentrated on the rhythm, a troubling thought kept cropping up in the back of her mind.

For all her mother said about wanting to get away, wanting to relax, Trina had a pretty good idea why her mother was really staying on.

She didn't want to be alone. That was why. Her mother didn't want to go back to an empty apartment, filled with sad memories. Trina could picture her there, lonely, crying, feeling abandoned.

It all became very clear to Trina. Mrs. Sandburg might be putting on a cheerful face, but deep inside she was devastated by what Trina had told her. The one man she loved had found someone new. She wanted to stay here because she needed to be with her daughter. She needed comfort and companionship.

Trina made a sudden decision. She couldn't let her mother suffer alone like that. When her mother left to go home, Trina would leave with her. She'd cut her camp vacation short and go back home.

It wouldn't be easy. She'd miss camp. She'd miss the fun and the sports and of course all her friends, especially Katie. But she'd make the sacrifice for her mother. It was the least she could do to make up for her father's desertion.

Should she tell her now? No, her mother would just try to talk her out of it. She'd wait and tell her when the time was right.

There was a bump as they hit the shore. "We won! We won!" Mrs. Sandburg yelled.

Trina grinned. It was so wonderful to see her mother happy.

* * *

All the girls were especially exhausted as they got ready for bed that night. "It'll be nice to have a normal day tomorrow," Katie said.

"Yeah," Erin agreed. "I was glad to see my parents. But I wasn't all that sorry to see them leave."

There were general echoes of agreement, but not from Trina. "My mother's staying in Pine Ridge for a few days."

Sarah was coming out of the bathroom. "My father's hanging around for a while too. He's got something to do in Pine Ridge."

"That's nice," Trina said sleepily. "Maybe we can all have dinner together in town."

Whispered calls of good night floated across the room. Hearing their voices, Trina thought about how much she'd miss them all. But her mother's happiness came first.

Chapter 4

"What time does the bus leave for Pine Ridge?" Erin asked when they came back to the cabin after archery the next day.

"About half an hour," Katie said. "Trina, are you going to see your mother?"

"Of course," Trina replied. "I figured I'd have lunch with her, and then we'd just walk around Pine Ridge and spend the day together."

"You're going to spend the whole day with her?" Katie asked in surprise. "We're all planning to go to the movies this afternoon, remember?"

"There's going to be a movie on the lake tonight," Trina pointed out.

"Yeah, but this is the new Rod Laney movie

51

and this is the last day it's playing. The one that was filmed right here at Sunnyside."

"The one *I* was in," Megan added, hopping up and down. "Oh boy, I can't believe I'm going to see myself right up there on the big screen."

Erin sniffed. "You were just an extra, Megan. We probably won't even be able to see you in the crowd."

The other girls hid their smiles. Erin had schemed and connived to get herself in the film, but to no avail. For two days, she'd been a stand-in for one of the stars, but that had been a disaster.

"I can see it another time," Trina said. "Look, my mother's staying here just to see me. I *have* to spend the day with her. Besides, I want to." She turned to Sarah. "You're spending the day with your father, right?"

"Well, not the whole day," Sarah said. "I guess we'll have lunch, but after that I'm going to the movie. My father's got things to do anyway." She glanced at the clock. "I better go call and tell him when I'm coming. Anyone want to go to the phone with me?"

"I'll come," Trina said. "I should call my mother too. We'll meet you guys at the bus."

The two girls walked across the camp to the

activities hall where the phone was. "It's weird, having a parent here at camp," Sarah commented.

"But it's nice," Trina said. "It's a change from just hanging out with the girls."

"I like hanging out with the girls," Sarah said mildly.

"So do I. But think about how happy it will make your father having you with him. He's probably been miserable at home without you."

"I doubt that," Sarah said. "I mean, I'm sure he misses me and all that. But he doesn't depend on me to be happy."

She must not be as close to her father as I am to my mother, Trina thought. Maybe that was because Sarah had a sister and Trina was an only child.

Luckily, nobody else was using the telephone in the activities hall. "Do you want to call first?" Sarah asked.

"No, you go ahead," Trina said. "They're both staying at the Pine Ridge Inn, right? Here's the number."

Sarah dialed. "Dr. Fine, please." She waited a moment. "Hi, Dad, it's me. I'm coming into town on the camp bus. Do you want to eat lunch with me?" There was a pause, and then she said,

"Great, I'll meet you at the inn. I have to go now, Trina wants to call her mother. She is? Okay."

Sarah held the phone out to Trina. "Your mother's right there."

Trina blinked. "In your father's room? What's she doing there?"

Sarah gave an I-don't-know shrug, and Trina took the phone. "Hello, Mom?"

"Hi, darling. What's up?"

"Um, I just wanted to tell you I'd be there in about half an hour. There's a little restaurant called the Country Place on Main Street. Do you want to meet me there?"

"Sounds lovely," her mother said.

"I wonder why she was there," Trina murmured as she replaced the receiver.

"They probably saw each other at breakfast and started talking," Sarah said.

That could be true, Trina thought. Her mother was so lonely, she'd talk to anyone, even some doctor she had nothing in common with. They left the activities hall and went to join the others in front of the dining hall, where the bus was waiting.

"I can't *wait* to see this movie," Katie said as they boarded. "Rod Laney, what a hunk!"

"And to think we actually met him in person." Sarah sighed in ecstasy.

"Which you owe to me," Erin pointed out. "If I hadn't asked him for his autograph for Katie, he'd never have come over to cabin six."

"We've already thanked you a zillion times," Katie said. "It's going to be so neat seeing Sunnyside in a movie."

"Not to mention seeing *me*," Megan piped up.

Trina couldn't help feeling a slight touch of envy as she listened to them. It *would* be neat, recognizing all the familiar places on the screen. Oh well, she'd just have to wait until next year when the movie came out as a video.

It was a short ride into the village of Pine Ridge. "Where are you guys going to be?" Sarah asked when they got off on Main Street.

"We'll grab a hamburger at Burger Bonanza," Katie said, "and then go straight to the theater. The movie starts at two, so why don't you meet us in front of the theater."

"Have a good time," Trina told them. "I guess I'll see you back at the bus."

Katie looked at her with regret. "Well, if you get tired of being with your mother, you know where we'll be."

Trina nodded, but she knew that wasn't

likely. They all took off, and she went in the opposite direction. She walked quickly, figuring that her mother was probably sitting in the restaurant, anxiously awaiting her.

A woman standing just inside the Country Place smiled at her. "May I help you?"

"I'm meeting my mother here," Trina said. Her eyes scanned the room. "I guess she's not here yet."

"I'll seat you over here, where you can watch for her," the woman said. She led Trina to a little table set for two, and placed two menus down.

Trina glanced at the clock. It was a little more than half an hour since she'd spoken to her mother, maybe five minutes. Of course, Mrs. Sandburg did have a tendency to be late, but Trina thought that this time her mother would be so eager to be with her daughter, she'd be on time.

Then the restaurant door opened, and her mother came in. She spotted Trina, waved, and hurried over to the table. "Am I late, darling? I'm sorry," she said, sitting down. Her face was flushed with excitement, and she looked as happy as Trina could ever remember seeing her. And all because I'm with her, Trina thought.

Her commitment to go home became even stronger.

Impulsively, she reached across the table and squeezed her mother's hand. "Mom . . . when you go back home, maybe I'll come with you."

Her mother's eyebrows shot up. "You mean, leave Sunnyside? But, Trina, why?"

Trina had to think. If she told her mother the real reason, she'd never let Trina leave. "I don't know. I guess I just want to come home."

"I don't understand! You always have such a wonderful time here!"

The waitress came to take their orders. Even as she told the waitress what she wanted, Mrs. Sandburg's curious eyes never left Trina's face.

"Tuna salad and a Coke, please," Trina said.

"Now, what's all this about leaving Sunnyside," Mrs. Sandburg asked. "From your letters, you sound like you're having the best summer yet."

"Actually," Trina said slowly, "it hasn't been all that wonderful."

"No?"

"Well, Katie's been so bossy. And . . . and we do the same things every day. It gets boring." She wished the food would come so she'd have something to look at besides her mother's concerned face. It was hard for her to lie.

"That's not what you were saying yesterday."

Trina shifted around uncomfortably in her seat. "All I'm saying is I wouldn't mind coming home."

The food appeared, but Mrs. Sandburg didn't pick up her fork. She was leaning across the table and studying Trina with a serious expression. "Trina, something's bothering you. Now, I want you to tell me what it is. Does it have something to do with your father?"

"No . . ."

"Then what?"

She could tell from her tone that her mother wasn't going to give up until Trina provided her with a satisfactory answer. And the only one she could think of was the truth. "I know you're lonely at home, Mom. I feel like I should be there to keep you company."

"Darling, I'm not lonely! I've got my friends and my work, and I'm perfectly content. In fact, I'm very happy right now, because I've just come up with a fabulous new project, an article I'm really excited about. There's absolutely no reason for you to go home with me."

The surprise must have been evident on Trina's face, because she quickly added, "Of course, I miss you very much. But what would you do at home? I'd be writing all day." She smiled. "It's sweet that you're so concerned, but you shouldn't be. I'm having a good summer, just like you are."

She's too proud to admit the truth, Trina decided. Maybe she'd better change the subject and not bring it up again until just before her mother left. "There's a movie on the lake tonight at camp. Do you want to come?"

"Love to," her mother said promptly. They ate their lunch, and Mrs. Sandburg filled her in on the neighborhood news. When they finished, her mother left money on the table for the bill, and they got up.

"What do you want to do now?" Trina asked.

"I was going back to the inn to work," her mother said. "They have a lovely garden, and I was planning to sit there and write. Aren't you meeting your friends?"

"Um, I guess I could," Trina stuttered. "But I thought *we'd* spend the day together."

"Well, we can, if you'd like," Mrs. Sandburg said. "But why would you want to hang around with your old mother when you can be with your friends?"

"I thought you wouldn't have anything else to do."

Mrs. Sandburg laughed merrily. "Nonsense. To tell you the truth, I'm dying to get back to work on this article. You run off and find your friends, and I'll see you tonight at camp."

It was only one-thirty, so Trina walked slowly toward Pine Ridge's one and only movie theater. She needed time to think anyway. She found it hard to believe her mother could be so excited about her work. Why, just yesterday, she'd been complaining about how boring it had been lately. She was probably just saying that so Trina wouldn't feel duty bound to stay with her all day.

The others were in line at the ticket booth when Trina got to the theater. A pleased smile crossed Katie's face as she waved to her, and then she turned away to stare in awe at the poster of Rod Laney advertising the movie.

"Yay, here's Trina!" Megan squealed. "I wanted us all to see this together!"

"How come you didn't stay with your mother?" Erin asked.

"She said she had something to do," Trina murmured. She turned to Sarah. "Did you have a nice lunch with your father?"

"Sure. It was fine."

Katie actually tore her eyes from the Rod Laney poster. "You don't look like you had a very good time."

"Oh, I did," Trina said. "I guess I'm just worried about my mother being alone all day."

"Oh, Trina, that's silly," Sarah said. "She's a grown-up. I'm sure she's got her own plans, just like my father."

"Yeah, you worry too much," Megan echoed.

Trina gazed at them all in annoyance. Why couldn't they understand? "I told her I'd go home with her when she leaves," she blurted out.

They all stared at her in horror. "Leave Sunnyside?" Katie gasped. "In the middle of the summer? That's crazy! Why would you do a thing like that?"

Trina groaned in exasperation. "Because my mother's all alone at home. She *needs* me."

Sarah put her hands on her hips and eyed Trina sternly. "Trina, did she *ask* you to come home?"

"No . . . in fact, she thinks I should stay here. She *says* she's happy at home, but I don't believe her."

"Of course she's happy," Katie said impatiently. "Like Sarah said, she's a grown-up. She's got her own life."

No, they'd never understand, Trina thought. Their parents had each other, or, like Sarah's father, another child. She was all her mother had. "I invited her to come to the movie on the lake tonight."

"I told my father about it too," Sarah said, "but I don't think he'll come. I told him the movies were usually pretty dumb, and he's not the type to sit outside on the ground."

They bought their tickets and went inside. Arming themselves with popcorn and sodas, they hurried to find good seats toward the front. While the others giggled in anticipation, Trina halfheartedly munched on some popcorn and stared at the dark screen. What was her mother doing right that minute? Probably sitting in that garden and feeling sad. And what was her father doing? Probably having a merry time with his girlfriend. She could feel her mouth set in a tight line. It was all his fault that her mother was sad and Trina had to feel so bad about it.

The lights went down, the screen lit up, and the movie began. Despite all her troublesome thoughts, Trina found herself getting caught up in the movie right away. It was a great story about a counselor, played by Rod Laney, and his romance with a lifeguard at a summer camp. They'd been in love when they were in college together, but they'd broken up. At first, when they saw each other at camp, they didn't speak. But they finally came together when a camper ran away, and they both went looking for her.

The camper was played by Tish, who Erin had tried to become friendly with in order to get into the movie. Seeing her act like an angry, spoiled brat reminded the cabin six girls how nasty Tish had been in real life.

Every time Tish appeared on the screen, Erin made a face. "You would have been better in that part," Trina whispered to her. It was just a little white lie to make Erin feel better.

"I know," she whispered back.

In the movie, the place was called Camp Friendship, but it was definitely Sunnyside.

Each time a familiar sight came into view—the pool, the lakefront, the activities hall—the girls clutched each other and Katie let out a little whoop.

"There I am!" Megan screeched.

"Shh," someone hissed behind them, but they paid no attention. There was only a glimpse of

Megan's freckled face and red curls in a crowd scene, but it was still neat to see her. Trina recognized some of the other extras too. And even though she herself wasn't in the movie, it was exhilarating to think that all over the country people would be seeing *her* camp and one of her cabin mates in the movies.

When the movie was over and the lights came up, the girls just sat there for a moment, still in a daze. "That was wonderful," Katie sighed.

"Do you think anyone will recognize me?" Megan asked, looking around.

No one seemed to, but that didn't bother her. "In a way, we're all famous now," Sarah mused as they left. "Sunnyside was the real star of that movie, and we're all Sunnyside girls. Trina, you *can't* leave."

The same thought had been creeping into Trina's head. But her mind conjured up the image of her mother sitting alone with a woebegone face, and that pushed the thought away.

"We've got time to get ice cream before the bus leaves," Katie said. The girls headed toward the ice cream shop. They were just passing the Pine Ridge Inn when Sarah stopped suddenly and poked Trina. "Look!"

Through the green hedge that surrounded the

inn, Trina could see into the garden. There was her mother, just as she'd said she would be. But she wasn't working, and she wasn't alone.

Dr. Fine was with her. He was talking, and although Trina couldn't hear what he was saying, she could see her mother smiling and nodding. Then a waitress appeared by their little table. She placed a teapot and a plate of little cakes between them.

Dr. Fine must have said something funny, because Mrs. Sandburg's smile broadened, and her tinkling laugh pierced the hedge.

"What are they doing?" Trina wondered out loud.

"Keeping each other company, I guess," Sarah replied.

Trina frowned slightly. "*I* would have had tea with her if she'd asked me."

"Sometimes grown-ups just want to be with other grown-ups," Sarah said. "C'mon." The others had walked on ahead.

Trina hesitated. "Maybe I should go join her."

"Why?" Sarah asked. "They're doing fine on their own. Let's go." Trina took one last peek through the hedge before hurrying to catch up with the others.

That just proves my point, she thought. No

matter how much her mother denied it, she was lonely. Otherwise, why would she be spending time with Sarah's father? She had an awful vision of her mother back home, roaming the town in search of someone, anyone, to talk to. She shuddered. Somehow, she had to get her mother to let her leave.

The movie on the lake that night wasn't anywhere near as good as the one they'd seen that afternoon. It was a silly story about a widowed man and a widowed woman who got married. The man had two daughters, the woman had two sons, and they fought all the time. Of course, by the end, they were one big happy family.

"This is really corny," Katie mumbled to Trina, and Trina agreed. She turned to see how her mother, sitting behind her, was reacting.

She wasn't even watching. She and Dr. Fine had their heads together and they were talking softly.

Sarah had been surprised when her father showed up at the lake. She too kept turning and looking back at him.

When the movie was over, Trina got up and

turned to her mother. "I'll walk you to your car."

"That's all right," her mother said, smiling. "I came with Dr. Fine in his car." She bent down and kissed Trina's forehead. "I'll see you tomorrow. Ms. Winkle said I could come over and have lunch with you kids."

"Great," Trina said.

Dr. Fine ruffled Sarah's head. "I'll be over here too."

As the two adults walked away, Trina gazed after them thoughtfully. She realized Sarah was watching them too.

"They're certainly spending a lot of time together," Trina noted.

"Yeah," Sarah replied.

There was a moment of silence between them. The two girls looked at each other. And then, very quickly, they looked away.

Chapter 5

Trina was running down a long, dimly lit corridor. Everywhere she looked, there were hallways going in different directions. She knew she was looking for something, but she didn't know what. A man appeared at the end of one hallway. "Daddy!" she yelled. "I'm here!" But he was arm in arm with a woman and didn't even hear her. She kept on running. "Mom! Where are you? Mom!" And then she saw her. But she too was arm in arm with a figure in a long white coat. "Mom! Come back!" But they kept on walking away from her. "Mom! Mom!"

"Trina! Wake up!"

The familiar voice was ringing in the back of her head and slowly began to penetrate. She felt hands on her shoulders, shaking them.

Trina opened her eyes and stared blankly into Katie's. "What—what's going on?"

"You were dreaming!"

Trina sat up. "I was?"

Katie was looking at her in wonderment. "I guess you were having a nightmare. You kept calling 'Daddy' and 'Mom.'"

Trina stared right back at her. "I don't have nightmares."

"You did just now," Katie insisted.

Embarrassed, Trina looked around the cabin. Everyone else was still sleeping, thank goodness.

"Are you okay?" Katie asked anxiously.

Trina rubbed her forehead. "I'm fine. I don't even know what I was dreaming about."

"Yeah, that happens to me sometimes," Katie said. "I'll know I had a bad dream, but I won't remember what it was. Go back to sleep."

Trina nodded and sank back on her pillow. What *was* she dreaming about? But she fell asleep before she could figure that out.

When she woke up the next morning, she felt pretty groggy. Around her, the girls were rising and moving about the cabin getting dressed. Trina got out of her bed and stumbled toward the bathroom. Just as she reached it, the door swung open and Sarah almost collided with her.

"Good grief!" Trina exclaimed in annoyance. "Watch where you're going, Sarah!"

Sarah was taken aback. "Well, *excuse me!*"

Trina suddenly became aware that Megan, Erin, and Katie were all looking at her strangely. And she couldn't blame them. It wasn't like her to snap at anyone that way. "I'm sorry," she murmured and went on into the bathroom.

She looked at herself in the mirror. What was wrong with her, anyway? She splashed some water on her face and felt a little better.

When she went back out into the cabin, Sarah was telling Carolyn that her father was coming over to Sunnyside for lunch.

"That's nice," Carolyn said. "Trina, is your mother coming too?"

Trina nodded as she began dressing.

"Are they coming together?" Megan asked.

"I don't know," Trina said. "Why?"

Megan's eyes twinkled mischievously. "It just seems to me that they've been spending all their time together since they came to Sunnyside."

71

"What's *that* supposed to mean?" Sarah asked sharply.

"Nothing," Megan said, her face all innocence.

"Hurry up, girls, it's almost time for breakfast," Carolyn said and went back into her own room.

"I think it's cool," Erin commented.

"What's cool?" Katie asked.

"Mrs. Sandburg and Dr. Fine. It's cool the way they got together."

Trina paused in the process of tying her shoelaces. "What's so special about that?"

"They must like each other a lot to spend all this time with each other," Erin said.

Megan's face took on that glazed expression that meant her imagination was at work. "I wonder if it's more than liking each other. After all, he doesn't have a wife and she doesn't have a husband. Maybe they took one look at each other on Parents' Day, and boom!"

"What do you mean, 'boom'?" Trina asked in a weak voice. But she knew what Megan's answer would be. That was why she was getting this awful jumpy, queasy feeling in her stomach, why she had the nightmare last night, why she had snapped at Sarah that morning.

72

Megan placed a hand over her heart. "They could be falling madly in love."

"Megan!" Sarah's face was a sickly pale color. Trina suspected her own face was the same shade.

"Well, it's not impossible," Megan said. "Think about it. Wouldn't that be something, if they fell in love and got married? Sarah and Trina would be sisters!"

Katie's eyes darted between Trina, Sarah, and Megan. Then she spoke briskly. "Get off your cloud, Megan. You're being ridiculous."

"Why is it ridiculous?" Erin asked. "It happened in the movie last night."

"It was a dumb movie," Katie stated with authority. "And stuff like that doesn't happen in real life."

Trina smiled at her gratefully. "Katie's right. It's a silly idea, Megan."

"Very silly," Sarah echoed. But she didn't look at Trina, and Trina didn't look at her.

When the girls gathered at their table for lunch in the dining hall that afternoon, Trina and Sarah did exchange quick looks. As if by unspoken agreement, they took seats at the opposite ends of the table. At least that would force a temporary separation of their parents.

They did come in together. Of course, that was probably just for convenience, Trina told herself. It would be silly for them each to take a car when they were both coming to the same place.

"C'mon, Dad," Sarah said, grabbing her father's arm. "Let's get our lunch."

Mrs. Sandburg breezed over to Trina, planted a quick kiss on her forehead, and announced, "I'm starving."

Trina glanced at the line which had formed for the lunch trays. Luckily, at least three people had followed Sarah and Dr. Fine, so they wouldn't be directly behind them.

"It's a good lunch today," she told her mother as they went to the line. "Macaroni and cheese."

"My favorite!" Mrs. Sandburg exclaimed. "Trina, I'm having such a nice time here. Everything is just perfect."

Trina smiled nervously. Her mother seemed even more cheerful than she usually behaved. Trina had a sinking suspicion that her happy mood wasn't entirely due to being with her daughter. Could Megan be right? Could something romantic actually be happening between her mother and Dr. Fine?

All through lunch, she observed her mother carefully for any signs of being in love. She watched to see if she exchanged any secretive winks or smiles with Dr. Fine at the other end of the table.

"Trina, is there something on my face?" Mrs. Sandburg asked in an undertone. "Did I drip cheese on my chin?"

"No," Trina said. "You look fine. Why?"

"You're staring at me in such a peculiar way."

Trina felt her face redden. "I guess I'm just thinking about how much I'll miss you when you leave."

Her mother laughed. "Nonsense. You'll go right back to having the same good times you had before I came." She gave Trina a meaningful look, and Trina knew what it meant. There was no way she'd let Trina go home with her.

Trina's eyes darted down the table toward Dr. Fine. But he was deep in conversation with Sarah and Carolyn, and not even attempting to talk to her mother. That was a relief. It's all in Megan's crazy imagination, Trina thought. But she still wanted to get her mother alone so she could find out for sure.

She checked the clock on the wall. There was still some time left before the lunch period was over, and her mother seemed to have finished. Trina herself wasn't very hungry. "Carolyn, could I take my mother for a walk?"

"Sure," Carolyn said. "Just be back in the cabin for rest period, okay?"

"I'd like a walk," Mrs. Sandburg said, rising from her chair. Then she turned to Dr. Fine. "I'll meet you back here in fifteen minutes."

Sarah's father smiled and nodded. Trina couldn't decide if it was just a nice, polite smile or if it meant something more. Once outside, she tried to think of a way to bring up the topic on her mind.

Her mother spoke first. "I wish I didn't have to leave tomorrow."

"Couldn't you stay a few more days?" Trina asked.

"No, darling. I've got a meeting with an editor."

They walked along in silence for a few minutes. "Mom, what did you think of that movie last night?"

"To tell you the truth, Trina, I wasn't paying

much attention to it. I was talking to Martin, and—"

"Martin?"

"Dr. Fine."

"Oh." So now they were on a first name basis. She was dying to ask her what they had been talking about, but she didn't dare. She was afraid of what the answer might be.

Just then, Mrs. Sandburg clapped a hand to her mouth. "Oh dear, I knew I forgot something."

"What's that?"

"I want to ask Ms. Winkle if you can come into Pine Ridge tonight to have dinner with me, since it will be my last night here."

Trina brightened. At least her mother wanted to spend this last night with *her.* "That will be fun," she said.

Her mother nodded happily. "And Martin is going to ask if Sarah can come too."

Trina's heart sank. "Oh, that's nice," she managed to say. Her mother didn't seem to notice the change in tone.

"I'd better run back right now and ask her. I'll see you later, Trina." And she ran back toward the dining hall.

Trina started to walk slowly and stiffly back

77

to cabin six. That queasy feeling had returned to her stomach. And in her mind, strange and frightening pictures were forming. She saw her mother back home, alone. She heard the phone ringing. It was Dr. Fine, asking her for a date. The Fines didn't live that far from the Sandburgs, only about two hours. It wouldn't be hard for them to travel back and forth.

Then she saw herself returning from camp, to be greeted by the news that her mother and Sarah's father were to be married. She envisioned their small apartment invaded by Sarah, her sister, and her father. Or maybe she and her mother would move to the Fines' home. Trina would have to leave her school, her friends, the town where she'd lived all her life. . . .

It was too much to bear. Her eyes were stinging. Stop it, she told herself fiercely. You're getting worse than Megan with all this daydreaming.

But the images wouldn't leave her. She had to do something. Maybe she could write to her father. Maybe it wasn't too late for them to get back together.

Her pace quickened, and she hurried back to the cabin. The others were arriving back from lunch.

"Okay, girls, settle down," Carolyn told them. "Oh, Trina, there's a letter for you." Trina took the envelope and saw her father's return address in the corner.

"I have to go see someone," Carolyn said. "You guys are on your honor to be quiet, got it?"

Katie raised her right hand. "We promise." And then, deliberately, she turned so Carolyn could see her crossed fingers behind her back.

"Very funny," Carolyn said dryly. She shook her head in amused resignation and walked out.

"Megan, have you seen the book I was reading?" Sarah asked.

"No," Megan replied.

"Trina, did you see it?"

"No," Trina said. "What would I be doing with your silly book?"

"I was just asking," Sarah said. "You don't have to get so nasty."

"I'm not being nasty," Trina retorted. "I'm just answering your question." She went to her bunk and tore open the envelope.

"Dear Trina," the letter began. "It was wonderful seeing you at camp. And I'm glad you and Shelly had the opportunity to meet. Shelly was very impressed with you, and I hope you felt the same about her. I want you two to get to know each other."

There was more to the letter, but Trina didn't want to read it. Gritting her teeth, she crumpled the paper and tossed it on the floor.

"What's that?" Katie asked. "The letter you got?"

"It's nothing important," Trina said. "Throw it in the wastebasket, okay?"

Katie picked the paper up from the floor and tossed it. It landed neatly in the basket. "Two points," she announced. "Who was it from?"

"My father," Trina said glumly. "I think he wants to get married."

"How awful!" That came from Sarah, lying on her bunk across the room.

Trina looked at her evenly. "No kidding."

"What's so awful about it?" Erin asked. "People *should* get married."

"That depends," Sarah replied, "on who they marry." Even though her words were directed at Erin, her eyes were still on Trina.

Across the room, Erin was watching them. "What are you two doing? Having a staring contest?"

Trina didn't answer. Neither did Sarah. Katie

looked at Trina. Then she looked at Sarah. "What's the matter with you two?"

"Nothing," Sarah said.

And Trina shook her head.

"Something's going on," Katie said. "I think you guys need cheering up. Maybe we should plan something special to do tonight after dinner."

"I won't be here," Sarah said. "Neither will Trina. We're having dinner with our parents in Pine Ridge."

Megan started giggling.

"What's so funny?" Trina asked.

"The way she said 'our parents.' Maybe they really will end up being both your parents."

"Oh, shut up, Megan!" Trina shouted.

And at the same time, Sarah yelled, "Forget it!"

The room fell deadly silent. Katie looked shocked, Erin's mouth had fallen open, and Megan's face was white. Trina got out of her bunk and ran into the bathroom.

A moment later, Sarah came in. "What do you want?" Trina asked.

Sarah took a deep breath. "I think we'd better talk about this."

They eyed each other warily. Trina broke the

silence with a whispered question. "Do you think it's true? That they're falling in love?"

"I'm not sure," Sarah said. But the worried look in her eyes told Trina she was afraid of the very same thing.

"I don't want my mother to get married," Trina said. "Nothing personal. I mean, I'm sure your father is a very good person. But I've already lost my father. I can't lose my mother too."

Sarah nodded. "Your mother's very nice, but I don't want my father getting married either."

"What are we going to do?" Trina asked.

"I don't know." Sarah began chewing on a fingernail.

Then the bathroom door opened and Katie walked in. "I've never heard either of you yell like that before. What's this all about?"

"We're scared that Megan's right about our parents," Sarah said. "And neither of us wants them to get married."

"We don't know what to do about it," Trina said. She looked at Katie hopefully. Katie was always so good at coming up with ideas.

"Just don't let that happen," she said.

"But how can we stop it?" Sarah asked.

Katie considered the problem. "Let me think

about it." She gave them a reassuring smile. "I promise, by the end of rest period, I'll have a solution for you."

The confidence in her voice made Trina feel better, and Sarah looked calmer too. "Thanks," they chorused.

They lingered in the bathroom after Katie left.

"Katie's come up with some brilliant schemes before," Trina noted.

"I know," Sarah said. "But I can remember some others that turned out to be disasters."

She was right, and Trina knew that. "But I'll try just about anything to stop them from getting together."

"Me, too," Sarah said. She held out her right hand. Trina held out her's, and they shook hands.

At least now they were in this together.

Chapter 6

"Now, are you two going to remember everything I told you?" Katie asked. With her stern expression and her hands on her hips, she looked like an army general sending her troops into battle. Of course, army generals usually didn't give their commands in a bathroom.

"Ouch!" Sarah yelped as Erin tried to brush a snarl out of her hair. "Yeah, yeah, I'll remember."

"What about you, Trina?"

"I'll remember." Trina hesitated. "But I'm just not sure that I can pull this off."

Megan, perched on a sink, nodded. "You know how everyone can tell when Trina's lying."

"You won't really be lying," Katie told Trina. "Just exaggerating."

"And my father doesn't know you well enough to tell when you're lying," Sarah pointed out.

"I guess that's right," Trina said, her tone carrying the doubt she was feeling. "But what about my mother? *She'll* know if I'm lying."

"Just be careful," Katie advised. "Like I said, you don't really have to lie. All you have to do is point out the differences between your mother and Sarah's father. People can't get married if they're that different."

"And they really are different," Megan said. "If everything you guys have told us is true."

"It's all true," Trina affirmed.

"Look," Sarah said, "if this means as much to you as it does to me, you'll find a way to pull it off."

Erin continued to tug at Sarah's hair. "Personally, if you want my opinion . . ."

Trina didn't, but she knew Erin would give it whether she wanted it or not.

Erin continued. "I think you're both being very silly and immature, trying to break them up. And I think Katie's idea is dumb."

Trina considered this. Yes, it was silly and immature. And maybe the idea was dumb. But Katie's plan was better than anything *she* could come up with. And Sarah was right. It did mean a lot to her.

She glanced in the mirror. Her lips were pressed together so tightly they were white.

"How are you getting to Pine Ridge?" Katie asked.

"My father's picking us up," Sarah replied.

"Good," Katie said. "That means Trina can get started playing her part right away."

Trina felt sick. It was one thing to go along with a scheme. It was something else to have to *get* it going.

They all left the bathroom. In the cabin, Carolyn was waiting to escort the others to dinner in the dining hall. She looked over Sarah and Trina in their best dresses, and nodded with approval. "You both look lovely. Have a wonderful time."

"And good luck," Megan added.

Carolyn's brow furrowed. "What do they need good luck for?"

Sarah glared at Megan fiercely.

Megan gave her a lame smile. "Uh, I don't know. Good luck in, um, picking something good from the menu, I guess."

Sarah and Trina hurried out before Carolyn could pursue that strange remark. In silence, they walked over to the activities hall, where Dr. Fine was going to pick them up. Trina couldn't think of anything to say to her. They'd been so uncomfortable with each other since Parents' Day.

"Does this feel weird to you?" Sarah asked.

"Yeah," Trina replied. "Very weird."

"But it's the only way," Sarah noted.

Trina nodded. And they exchanged uncertain smiles.

"There's my father's car," Sarah said as they approached the activities hall.

"He's certainly punctual," Trina commented.

"Very punctual," Sarah declared. "In fact, that's a big deal with him. He hates when my sister and I dawdle or when we're late for something."

"Oh, yeah?" Trina filed that information away. It could be useful.

"Quick, before we get in the car, tell me something more about your mother," Sarah said.

Trina thought rapidly. "Well, she's kind of extravagant. She loves to spend money. She and my father used to argue about that a lot."

Sarah grinned. "Very interesting."

Dr. Fine tooted his horn and the girls waved.

Trina climbed into the backseat and Sarah got in the front. "Hello, girls," he said.

"Hello," Trina replied, and Sarah kissed his cheek. Dr. Fine beamed at them both before starting the car. He's got a nice smile, Trina thought. Her mother always did like people with big smiles.

"Were we late?" Sarah asked.

"No, I was early," Dr. Fine told her.

Sarah turned to face Trina. "Dad likes to get to places early. When he picks me up somewhere, he's always there five minutes before I told him to be there."

Trina took a deep breath. Here was a perfect opportunity to get things going. "That's the opposite of my mother. She's always late."

Sarah glanced at her father, as if to make sure he was listening. "Really?"

"Yeah. Once she was a whole hour late picking me up from school." Trina was glad she was in the backseat. Even if Dr. Fine didn't know her very well, she was glad he couldn't see her face when she said that. It was true that her mother tended to be late for things. But usually by only a few minutes, not a whole hour.

When Dr. Fine didn't respond to that, Sarah gave her an encouraging look, which clearly said "more." Trina thought rapidly. "She always misses the first few minutes of movies because she never gets there on time."

Sarah smiled broadly. "Boy, you'd hate that, wouldn't you, Dad?"

"Actually, I don't go to that many movies," her father said.

"My mother absolutely *loves* to go to the movies," Trina said. That wasn't really a lie, she told herself. Her mother did go to movies once in a while. And she never said she *didn't* like going to them.

By the time they arrived at the inn in Pine Ridge, Trina wondered if her comments were having any impact on Dr. Fine. He wasn't showing any reaction at all. But there was the meal yet to come, and at least she and Sarah had taken the first steps in pointing out how little Dr. Fine and Mrs. Sandburg had in common.

"Your mother's meeting us in the lobby," Dr. Fine said. But when they entered, she was nowhere in sight. Trina winked at Sarah, and said loudly, "See what I mean? She's never where she's supposed to be when she's supposed to be there."

Dr. Fine nodded absently and glanced at the stairway. "Ah, here she is."

Trina bit her lip. It was just her luck that this once her mother would be practically on time. As she watched her mother float down the stairs, Trina couldn't help understanding why a man like Dr. Fine might fall in love with her. She was so pretty, and her smile lit up her face. Trina steeled herself for the task ahead of them.

"Hello, everyone," Mrs. Sandburg greeted them. They all went into the dining room, where a man seated them at a table covered with linen and silver.

Dr. Fine was about to sit down when he patted his coat pocket. Then he uttered a mild groan. "I seem to have left my wallet in my room. Would you all excuse me for a minute?"

The moment he left, Sarah said, "Gee, I guess that means he's going to pay for this dinner. What a surprise."

Trina was prepared for this comment, and she knew what to say. "Why is that a surprise?"

"Because he's very cheap, normally. It's next to impossible for me to even get my allowance out of him. He's incredibly stingy."

Mrs. Sandburg laughed. "I've heard that before. I'll bet there's not a child in the world who doesn't think her parents are stingy."

"Mom, did you know Dr. Fine never goes to the movies?" Trina asked.

"He's not into doing fun things," Sarah added. "Work, work, work, that's all he ever does."

"Well, he does some very important work," Mrs. Sandburg murmured. She was studying the menu.

Dr. Fine returned to the table. "This is a terrific place," he said. "The cleaning service is incredible. When I changed clothes for this dinner, I was in such a hurry that I left a shirt on my bed. And it's already been picked up and put away in the closet."

"I know you must like that," Sarah said. "You want everything to be neat and tidy. What's that you always say, Dad? 'There's a place for everything, and everything should be in its place,' right?"

Trina turned to her mother. "I guess I can't say that about you, Mom, can I?"

"No kidding," Mrs. Sandburg agreed. "Trina's always nagging me to pick up after myself," she told the others.

Dr. Fine opened his menu. "I'd say it's the opposite in our house, right, Sarah?"

Sarah and Trina both ducked their heads and exchanged pleased, secret smiles. So far, so good.

A waiter came over. "May I take your orders?"

They gave their orders for dinner, and the waiter left. Then Dr. Fine said, "Sarah, if I forget, please remind me to call your sister after dinner."

"How old is your other daughter?" Trina's mother asked him.

"Alison's eighteen," he replied.

Trina felt Sarah's light kick under the table. "Uh, do you and Alison get along?" she asked Sarah.

Sarah gave a deep, heart-wrenching sigh and shook her head violently. "Never. We fight all the time. It's like constant warfare in our house."

Dr. Fine looked at her in astonishment. "How can you say that? You and Alison have always gotten along well."

"You just don't hear us," Sarah said. "We try not to argue in front of you."

"I'm glad I'm an only child," Trina remarked. "I wouldn't want any brothers or sisters."

Now it was Mrs. Sandburg's turn to look surprised. "Trina, that's not true. You always used to complain about being an only child."

"I've changed my mind," Trina said.

When the food came, Dr. Fine took a bite of his fish and smiled. "Ahh, just the right touch of basil."

"I don't recognize the herbs in my chicken," Mrs. Sandburg said.

"My father knows all about food," Sarah replied for him. "He's a gourmet cook."

Dr. Fine laughed. "Well, I don't know about being a gourmet, but I do enjoy cooking. It's my favorite way to relax."

"Then you've got lucky children," Mrs. Sandburg said. "Poor Trina has to suffer through my total lack of talent and interest in the kitchen."

Trina was about to protest and assure her mother that her cooking wasn't that bad, when she remembered her mission. "Mom's not into cooking," she said.

"That's an understatement," Mrs. Sandburg declared. "I never could see the point in putting a lot of effort into cooking. I mean, once it's eaten, it's gone!"

"True, it's a temporary satisfaction," Dr. Fine agreed. "But I take an enormous pleasure in a well-cooked meal."

The adults went on to debate the value of being a good cook. Trina and Sarah looked at each other in delight. Their parents were doing their work for them!

But after dinner, when Dr. Fine excused himself to call his other daughter, Trina didn't like the way her mother gazed after him with an appreciative smile.

"Your father's a very interesting man, Sarah," Mrs. Sandburg said.

Sarah shot Trina a worried look, and Trina frantically searched her mind for a new topic. "I had a letter from Dad today," she blurted out. "There was a lot about that girl, Shelly."

Her mother nodded. She was still staring at the door through which Dr. Fine had exited, and her eyes were sort of glazed. That meant she was thinking about something. Or someone. And Trina had a sinking sensation she knew who it was.

She forgot Sarah was sitting there with them. She tugged on her mother's sleeve. "Mom, I really think Dad might marry this Shelly."

"That's nice," her mother said.

"Nice! Mom, how can you say that? Don't you *mind?*"

The urgency in her voice got her mother's full attention. "No, Trina, I don't mind. I'm happy for him. And he'd be happy for me, if I was in

95

that situation." She turned to a window. "Oh my, what an incredibly gorgeous sunset. Let's go get a closer look."

She got up and went to a window. But Trina and Sarah didn't follow her. This time the looks they gave each other were full of dread.

"What's that supposed to mean?" Sarah asked. "Why would she be happy for him?"

Trina couldn't answer. She was afraid she knew what the reason was—that maybe her mother was planning something like marriage for herself.

She got up and joined her mother at the window. Mrs. Sandburg put an arm around her. "I'll stop by Sunnyside on my way home tomorrow. Where will you be around nine-thirty?"

"Arts and crafts," Trina replied. She could feel her heartbeat quicken. Was this when her mother was planning to break the news to her?

She was alarmed by the way her mother's eyes were gleaming. "You look awfully happy, Mom."

"I am. Look, there's Martin. Let's go back to the table." Feeling like her legs were made of lead, Trina managed to drag herself back.

"I guess we'd better get these girls back to

camp," Dr. Fine said. They left the inn and went to his car.

"Trina, it's been a pleasure getting to know you," he continued as they got into the car. Mrs. Sandburg got into the front seat next to Dr. Fine, but not too close, thank goodness. Maybe she was just trying not to be too obvious. Sarah and Trina got into the back.

As Dr. Fine pulled away, he added, "I'm glad you and Sarah are such good friends."

Trina couldn't bear to even look at her good friend. Was he saying that because the girls were soon going to be more than friends?

No one said much on the way out of Pine Ridge. Dr. Fine turned the radio on, and the strains of classical music filled the car. He hummed along.

"Do you like Mozart?" he asked Trina's mother.

"This is nice," she said. "But to be honest, I can't tell the difference between Mozart and Beethoven. I'm a rock and roll fan myself."

Dr. Fine uttered a groan. "How can you listen to that? It's just noise!"

This set off an argument in which Mrs. Sandburg staunchly defended the merits of rock music. For a moment, Trina felt a twinge of hope, and she held her breath.

But it was fleeting. "You know, this music is really lovely," her mother said. "I could get used to it."

Trina let her breath go out in a sigh. And Sarah slumped down in her seat.

But the worst was yet to come. As they pulled up in front of the activities hall, Mrs. Sandburg turned to Dr. Fine. "I wish we both could stay here longer. There's so much we still need to talk about."

"We could meet for breakfast tomorrow," he suggested.

"That would be great," she said. "Then we can get everything organized and set up some dates."

The expressions that Trina and Sarah now gave each other were ones of total despair. Somehow, they went through the motions of the good-byes. Then the car pulled away, and the girls started walking back to cabin six.

Trina had an enormous lump in her throat. She stole a sidelong look at Sarah. Her face was stony.

They walked halfway in silence. Finally, Sarah spoke. "I guess that's it."

"Yeah," Trina replied. She paused as the cabin came into view. "They're all going to want to know what happened."

Sarah stopped too. "Should we tell them?"

Trina thought about that. She could picture Katie's surprise, Megan's sympathy, Erin's "I told you so." She couldn't deal with all that yet. "No. Let's just say we did what Katie told us to do, and now we have to wait and see."

"Okay," Sarah said. They started walking again. But just as they reached the steps leading to the door, she stopped again. "But we know what's going to happen, don't we?"

Trina couldn't say "yeah," or "I know." All she could do was nod. She was afraid that her voice would break.

Chapter 7

Trina and Sarah tried to satisfy their cabin mates with a brief, casual description of the evening. But they weren't going to be put off that easily. As soon as lights were out and Carolyn had gone into her room, they all gathered on Trina's bed. Except for Sarah. She remained on her bunk above Megan's and pretended to be asleep. At least, Trina assumed she was pretending. She didn't see how Sarah could sleep if she was feeling anything like the way Trina was feeling.

"Tell us everything that happened," Megan urged Trina. "The whole story."

Trina squirmed. "Nothing happened. It was fine. I had roast beef."

101

Katie punched her shoulder lightly. "That's not what we want to hear and you know it. How did my plan work? What did you say to them?"

Sarah sat up in her bed. "Can't a person have any privacy around here?"

Erin uttered a short laugh. "In cabin six at Camp Sunnyside? No way."

"Look," Trina said in a tired voice, "we did what Katie told us to do. Now we just have to wait and see what happens."

"Something *did* happen," Katie insisted. "I can tell from your face."

She's bluffing, Trina thought. How could Katie see her expression in the dark?

Katie persisted. "Hey, this was my idea, and I'm entitled to know exactly what happened."

She wasn't going to give up, and Trina knew it. "Okay. I found out that Dr. Fine is very punctual, so I told him my mother's always late for everything. He said he doesn't go to movies much, so I said my mother loves movies. My mom is kind of extravagant, and Sarah told her that her father is cheap. Then they found out about a lot of things they don't have in common."

"Like what?" Erin asked.

"Well, he's neat and she's messy. He's into

food and she isn't. He listens to classical music and my mother listens to rock."

"This sounds good," Katie said in a pleased voice. "I knew it would work. I'll bet they ended up never wanting to see each other again."

"Not exactly," Trina said in a low voice.

And then Sarah spoke up in a flat voice. "They're having breakfast together tomorrow. They said they have things to organize and they want to make dates."

Erin broke the silence that greeted this announcement. "Well, I'm not surprised. After all, you know what they say. Opposites attract."

"Gee, that's right," Megan mused. "Maybe you guys made them like each other more than they did to begin with."

Katie groaned. "I never even considered that possibility. Wow, I'm sorry."

"Knock it off, you guys," Sarah muttered. "I'm trying to sleep."

"There must be something else you can do to stop them," Katie said. "Like, throw a tantrum."

"I've never thrown a tantrum in my life," Trina replied. "I wouldn't even know how to do it."

"I could teach you," Erin offered.

"No thanks."

"What about threatening to run away from home?" Megan suggested.

Trina shook her head. "My mother knows I'd never do anything like that."

"Shut up!" Sarah yelled.

Carolyn's door flew open. "Hey, you're all supposed to be in bed! Now!"

The girls scampered off Trina's bed and hurried to their own. Katie lingered a moment to give Trina's hand a pat. "I really am sorry," she whispered.

"Yeah," Trina whispered back, "but not half as sorry as I am."

Trina was the first in the bathroom the next morning. But she wasn't alone for long. Sarah came in. In silence, the girls brushed their teeth at side-by-side sinks.

"How many bathrooms do you have in your house?" Sarah asked suddenly.

"Just one," Trina replied. "And it's an apartment, not a house."

"We've got two," Sarah said. "One is just for my father. I have to share the other one with Alison. When do you take your bath at home? In the morning or at night?"

"Morning," Trina replied.

"You'll have to switch to night," Sarah told her. "Alison spends an hour in there every morning putting on her makeup and fixing her hair."

It annoyed Trina that Sarah was assuming they'd be living there after the marriage. "Who says we'll be moving to your house?"

"It must be bigger than your apartment," Sarah noted in a matter-of-fact tone.

"Probably," Trina said. "But who knows? Maybe they'll want to buy a new house."

"I doubt it. We just had our place painted, inside and out, and Dad had a porch built outside the back door. He loves that house. Besides, *I'm* not going to move away from my school and my friends."

"I don't want to move either," Trina told her.

"You won't have any choice," Sarah stated.

Trina busied herself replacing the cap on her toothpaste and walked back out into the bedroom.

When they all left for breakfast, Trina lagged behind the group. To her dismay, Sarah dropped back and joined her. "You won't have to bring your bed when you move. I already have two in my room."

Trina tried to shake off her bad feelings. Maybe Sarah had the right attitude. She might as well accept the inevitable and make the best of it. "What color is your bedroom?"

"Pink."

Trina shuddered. "I hate pink." She was amazed at how rude she sounded. But she couldn't help it. The idea of a pink bedroom gave her the creeps. "Maybe we can paint it."

"I don't want to paint it," Sarah objected. "I like pink. Besides, it's *my* room."

"Our room," Trina corrected her. "Do you use a flashlight to read under the covers like you do here?"

"No," Sarah replied. "I have a light on the nightstand by my bed."

Trina looked at her in alarm. "I can't sleep with a light on."

"Well, I can't go to sleep without reading for a while first. Are you as neat at home as you are here?"

"Yes."

"Great," Sarah moaned. "You'll make me look bad."

"I don't like messy bedrooms," Trina warned her.

"I hope you don't think I'm going to start

picking everything up just because you're Miss Tidy," Sarah retorted.

In the dining hall, Trina took a seat between Megan and Katie, so Sarah couldn't sit next to her. Unfortunately, the only seat left was directly across the table. To make matters worse, Carolyn wasn't in her usual place at the table. She had a counselors' meeting at another table, so the girls were free to say anything they wanted.

Trina picked at her food.

"These pancakes are great," Megan announced. "Trina, how come you're not eating?"

When Trina didn't say anything, Katie answered for her. "She never eats when she's upset."

"I'm the opposite," Sarah said, wolfing down her food. "I eat *more* when I'm upset."

"Sarah, you shouldn't talk with your mouth full," Trina reprimanded her.

"Since when can you tell me how I should talk?" Sarah fired back.

"Good manners never hurt anyone," Trina replied. She touched a napkin to her lips primly.

Sarah grimaced. "Look who's talking. You've got your elbows on the table."

Megan's eyes were fearful as they darted back

and forth between Sarah and Trina. "Um, Sarah, did you put my tee shirt on this morning? I couldn't find mine so I put on yours."

"I don't know," Sarah mumbled.

Erin, who was sitting beside her, reached over and looked in the neckline at the back of Sarah's tee shirt. "T. Sandburg," she read aloud from the label.

"Ha-ha," Katie uttered nervously. "I'll bet if we checked all our labels none of us would have our own on."

But Trina didn't think it was so funny. When they ended up living together, what else would Sarah take of hers? "I wish you wouldn't borrow my things without asking."

Sarah just scowled.

"And please have it washed before you give it back to me," Trina added.

Sarah's eyes narrowed. "What's the matter? Afraid you're going to get cooties?"

Megan's giggle sounded very forced. "This is crazy. Your parents aren't even married yet, and already you're fighting like sisters."

Trina shrugged and reached out her hand for a glass of orange juice.

"Hey, that's mine!" Sarah yelped and grabbed it. In the process, she knocked the glass over. A river of orange liquid trickled across the table and off it, landing on Trina's clean white shorts.

Trina leaped up. "Now look what you did!"

"It was an accident!" Sarah protested heatedly.

"She didn't mean to do that, Trina," Katie said in Sarah's defense, but Trina ignored her. She rubbed at the orange stain with a napkin, but that only spread it around and made it even worse.

"Oh, no," she wailed, "all my other shorts are in the laundry. And I'm going to see my mother in an hour."

"Big deal," Sarah snorted. "She's so spacey she won't even notice."

"Sarah!" Megan exclaimed.

Trina faced Sarah with fire in her eyes. "I can't believe you said that about my mother."

"But it's true, isn't it?" Sarah asked. Her eyes were blazing too. "You said so yourself. Personally, I don't know what my father sees in her."

"Yeah? Well, I don't know what my mother likes about your father!"

"He just happens to be a brilliant doctor," Sarah informed her coldly.

"So what? He's short, and he wears glasses,

and he doesn't have a whole lot of hair in case you didn't notice. My mother is beautiful."

"That's a matter of opinion."

"How dare you insult my mother?"

"You just insulted my father!"

"Trina, Sarah, stop it!" Katie cried out.

But there was only one way Trina knew to stop this fight. She threw down her napkin and stormed out.

Chapter 8

In the arts and crafts cabin, Trina halfheartedly tossed a few pieces of macaroni on her collage. Looking at the glued mishmash of beads, buttons, and assorted odds and ends, she thought about the various pieces of art she'd created that lined the walls of the kitchen back home. Would Dr. Fine want her collages on *his* walls? She doubted it. Not when he had two daughters of his own.

At the other end of the table, she heard Megan asking Sarah if her father was stopping by camp. "No," Sarah replied. "He had to leave right after breakfast. He has a big meeting with some other doctors back home." In a louder voice, she added, "He's a very important person, you know."

111

"My mother's coming here," Trina announced to no one in particular. "Even though she's got an important meeting with a newspaper editor." She gave Sarah a sidelong glance and a smug smile.

Katie, watching this little performance, edged closer to her. "Trina, you're not acting like yourself."

Trina's smile faded. "I know," she said miserably. She didn't feel like herself either. But then, nothing in her life was normal.

Erin was peering out the window. "Trina, here comes your mother."

Trina put her collage down. "Donna, can I go?"

The counselor, who busy helping another camper, waved an okay. Trina ran out of the cabin and met her mother. "How long can you stay?" she asked.

"Just a few minutes," Mrs. Sandburg said with regret. "But I had to see you before I left." She led Trina over to a bench, where they sat down. Then she gazed at Trina with an unusual intensity.

This is it, Trina thought in despair. She's going to tell me right now. She just hoped she could keep from bursting out in tears.

"Trina . . ." she began slowly.

This was like the time she'd told Trina about the divorce. It would take her forever to get the words out, and Trina wanted to get it over with. "Just say it, Mom." But before her mother could, tears welled up in Trina's eyes and began to stream down her face.

Mrs. Sandburg was taken aback. "Trina, what's the matter?"

"Oh, Mom, how could you do this to me?"

"Do what to you?"

Trina choked on her own words. "First Dad abandons me. And now you!"

"What do you mean? Trina, I'm not abandoning you. I'm just going home!"

"That's not what I'm talking about," Trina cried. "I mean, Dad and Shelly, you and Dr. Fine . . ."

Her mother looked totally confused. "What does Dr. Fine have to do with anything?"

"You're going to marry him!"

Mrs. Sandburg was momentarily speechless. "Marry . . . Dr. Fine?"

"Isn't that what you wanted to talk to me about?"

"Good grief, no! Whatever gave you that idea?"

Now Trina was totally confused. "Well, you've been spending so much time with him!"

Her mother's expression began to clear, the bewilderment replaced by sympathy and understanding. "And you thought . . . oh, Trina, that's not why we've been seeing each other. I've been interviewing him. He's involved in some fascinating medical research, and I'm going to write an article about it."

It took Trina a moment for what she was saying to sink in. When the message finally got through, a tingling sensation passed through her and she felt as if she could fly. All her worries and fears magically melted away. "Oh, Mom! Thank goodness! I'm so happy!"

Her mother smiled. But there were still lines of concern on her forehead.

"What *did* you want to talk to me about?" Trina asked.

"Your father."

Trina looked away. Mrs. Sandburg took Trina's chin in her hand and pulled her face back. "Honey, your father isn't abandoning you."

Trina grimaced. "I don't care about that anymore. As long as I've still got you. One parent's better than none."

"But you've still got two parents. Just because your father has a . . . a romance, doesn't mean he can't still love you. He does, very much. But he's got his own life to live too." After a moment, she added, "And so do I."

Trina gasped. "You mean, *you've* got a romance too?"

Mrs. Sandburg put an arm around her. "No, not at the moment. But someday, I may meet a special man. I might even want to marry him. But that won't effect my love for you." She paused. "Trina, it's not like you to be so selfish."

Trina's eyes widened. "Selfish? Me?"

Her mother nodded. "You can't have your parents all to yourself all the time, you know. You want us to be happy, don't you?"

"Of course I do," Trina replied fervently. "But don't I make you happy?"

"You make us both very happy. But parents may need more than the love of their child. We need other people in our lives too. I know that's not easy for you to accept. But parents are just regular people. And sometimes, they fall in love."

Trina's head was spinning. And then, it all started to make sense. "I guess I've only been thinking about myself."

Her mother kissed the top of her head. "And that's natural, at your age. It's hard for a child to think her parents may love someone else too. And if someone comes into my life, or your father's life, who makes us happy, then I hope you can be happy for us."

In a soft voice, Trina murmured, "I'll try."

"That's all I ask." Mrs. Sandburg stood up. "Walk me to my car?"

Trina did, and the good-byes they exchanged were even more loving than usual. She stood by the side of the road and waved until the car disappeared. Then she stood there for a moment, thinking. She was supposed to go right back to arts and crafts. But there was something she had to do first.

Cabin six was empty. Trina went to the wastebasket and poked through it. She pulled out a crumpled wad of paper and took it to the little desk, where she smoothed it out.

She reread the first paragraph, and this time, she went on to the second. "I know you're saddened by the fact that your mother and I are divorced. And I realize that it may be difficult for you when one of us has a new relationship. But always remember that no matter what happens, we'll never stop loving you. And try to understand that parents are people too. Love, Dad."

It was almost exactly what her mother had said. And Trina felt ashamed. She'd always considered herself to be mature and sensitive, the kind of person who paid attention to other people's feelings. But here she'd completely ignored the feelings of the two people she loved most in the world.

She took a sheet of paper and a pen, and started to write. "Dear Dad." That was as far as she got when the cabin door opened. She looked up. "Hi."

"Hi," Sarah replied. "I was looking for you."

"Yeah?"

Sarah sat down on the edge of Megan's bed, next to the desk. "Did you talk to your mother?"

Trina nodded.

"Did she tell you—you know?"

Trina shook her head. "Sarah, we've been really dumb."

"Huh?"

"They're not getting married."

Sarah's eyebrows rose above the rim of her glasses. "You talked her out of it?"

"I didn't have to. They were never having a

romance. She was just interviewing him for an article."

A deep sigh of relief escaped Sarah's lips. "Boy, I feel really stupid."

"So do I," Trina agreed. But for more reasons than that, she thought. Should she share with Sarah the conversation she'd had with her mother? she wondered. No, she decided. That was a conversation for Sarah to have with her own father.

Sarah got up. "I guess I'd better get back to arts and crafts."

"I'll go with you." She put the letter on her bed, with a mental promise to finish it later.

As they left the cabin, Trina found herself wanting to run or skip or hop all the way back. For the first time in days, she felt positively lighthearted. "You know," she said to Sarah, "I'm glad my mother didn't let me go home with her. I'd really miss this place. And the people."

"Including me?" Sarah asked.

Trina gave her an abashed smile. "Yeah. Including you."

"I'd miss you too," Sarah said promptly. "I wonder . . ."

"What?"

"Would it have been so bad being sisters?"

Trina thought about that. "Maybe not. We could have worked it out."

"I guess you're right," Sarah agreed. "But I'm perfectly happy to just stay campers. And cabin mates."

"And friends," Trina added.

The two girls gave each other the first absolutely real smile they'd exchanged in a long time. Then they linked arms and started to run.

A CAST OF CHARACTERS
TO DELIGHT THE HEARTS
OF READERS!

BUNNICULA　　　　　　51094-4/$2.95 U.S./$3.50 CAN.
James and Deborah Howe, illustrated by Alan Daniel
The now-famous story of the vampire bunny, this ALA
Notable Book begins the light-hearted story of the small
rabbit the Monroe family find in a shoebox at a Dracula
film. He looks like any ordinary bunny to Harold the dog.
But Chester, a well-read and observant cat, is suspicious
of the newcomer, whose teeth strangely resemble
fangs...

HOWLIDAY INN　　　　　69294-5/$3.50 U.S./$3.95 CAN.
James Howe, illustrated by Lynn Munsinger
The continued "tail" of Chester the cat and Harold the dog
as they spend their summer vacation at the foreboding
Chateau Bow-Wow, a kennel run by a mad scientist!

THE CELERY STALKS　　69054-3/$2.95 U.S./$3.50 CAN.
AT MIDNIGHT
James Howe, illustrated by Leslie Morrill
Bunnicula is back and on the loose in this third hilarious
novel featuring Chester the cat, Harold the dog, and the
famous vampire bunny.

NIGHTY-NIGHTMARE　　70490-0/$3.50 U.S./$3.95 CAN.
James Howe, illustrated by Leslie Morrill
Join Chester the cat, Harold the dog, and Howie the other
family dog as they hear the tale of how Bunnicula was
born while they are on an overnight camping trip full of
surprises!